Flicka, Ricka, Dicka
and the
BIG RED HEN

MAJ LINDMAN

ALBERT WHITMAN & COMPANY
Morton Grove, Illinois

The Snipp, Snapp, Snurr Books
Snipp, Snapp, Snurr and the Buttered Bread
Snipp, Snapp, Snurr and the Gingerbread
Snipp, Snapp, Snurr and the Red Shoes
Snipp, Snapp, Snurr and the Reindeer
Snipp, Snapp, Snurr and the Yellow Sled
Snipp, Snapp, Snurr Learn to Swim

The Flicka, Ricka, Dicka Books
Flicka, Ricka, Dicka and the Big Red Hen
Flicka, Ricka, Dicka and the Little Dog
Flicka, Ricka, Dicka and the New Dotted Dresses
Flicka, Ricka, Dicka and the Three Kittens
Flicka, Ricka, Dicka and Their New Friend
Flicka, Ricka, Dicka Bake a Cake

Library of Congress Cataloging-in-Publication Data
Lindman, Maj.
Flicka, Ricka, Dicka and the big red hen / Maj Lindman.
p. cm.
Summary: While caring for their aunt's chickens, three little
Swedish sisters are upset when the big red hen disappears.
ISBN 0-8075-2493-X
[1. Chickens—Fiction. 2. Sisters—Fiction. 3.Triplets—Fiction.
4. Farm life—Sweden—Fiction. 5. Sweden—Fiction.] I. Title.
PZ7.L659Fkd 1995   95-916
[E]—dc20   CIP
                                          AC

The text is set in 23' Futura Book
and 12' Bookman Light Italic.

A Flicka, Ricka, Dicka Book

They went to see Aunt Lotta's hens and rooster.

Flicka, Ricka, and Dicka were three little girls who lived in Sweden. They lived near Aunt Lotta. One day, they went to see her hens and rooster.

She had a name for each hen. The oldest hen was gray, and her name was Granny. The four white ones were named Dolly, Tolly, Poppy, and Rakel.

The sixth one was a big red hen. Her name was Maisie.

"She is smart," said Aunt Lotta. "She also lays golden brown eggs."

"How happy you must be to have all these chickens!" said Ricka.

"Yes, indeed," said Aunt Lotta. "But I cannot visit my sister because of them. If I go away for a long trip, who will care for the chickens?"

On their way home, Flicka, Ricka, and Dicka were busy thinking.

"Suppose," said Flicka, "that—"

"Suppose," said Ricka, "that we—"

"That we ask Father and Mother if we may take care of Aunt Lotta's chickens!" added Dicka, happily.

The girls told their parents about wanting to help Aunt Lotta.

Father said, "It is a fine idea to care for Aunt Lotta's chickens. But we will bring them here. I can fix the old garden shed for them."

The girls ran back to Aunt Lotta and told her about Father's idea. She agreed at once.

"I will write to my sister," she said, "and tell her I am coming."

Father said, "It is a fine idea."

In the morning, Father and the girls went to the garden shed.

"It will be a good house for the chickens," he said, "since it is near the bushes. They like to go under the branches. But we must clean up the shed first."

"I will carry away the old cans in this big box," said Ricka.

"I will sweep the floor," said Dicka.

Flicka held the nails while Father hammered. He made the hens' nests out of wooden boxes and filled them with straw.

Then he made the perch on which the chickens would roost.

At last the shed was ready.

Flicka held the nails while Father hammered.

The next day, Flicka, Ricka, and Dicka went to Aunt Lotta's house.

"We have come to take the hens and the rooster," said Flicka.

Ricka carried Dolly and Tolly. Dicka took Poppy and Rakel. Flicka carried Granny and Maisie. The hens flapped their wings and cackled. Then they were quiet.

Just as the girls were ready to leave, Maisie began to flap her wings again and almost got away.

"There now, Maisie," said Aunt Lotta. "Be calm so that Flicka can carry you."

When she heard Aunt Lotta, Maisie settled down, and the girls started for home.

Aunt Lotta brought the rooster.

Maisie began to flap her wings.

The hens seemed to like their new home. Even Maisie was peaceful.

But hens need lots of greens to eat.

Flicka, Ricka, and Dicka went out each day to gather dandelion leaves and other greens for them.

"I wonder which is more fun," said Flicka. "To go for long walks or to look for the hens' eggs."

"I like to walk and pick the fresh greens," said Dicka.

"It is fun to look for the eggs, too," said Ricka.

"We must hurry," said Flicka, "or the hens will be hungry."

"They are always hungry," said Dicka, laughing.

But hens need lots of greens to eat.

The rooster always crowed early in the morning.

"It is time to get up," said Ricka.

"I wonder how many eggs there will be," said Dicka.

The girls washed and dressed and ran to the chicken house.

Maisie, Granny, and two of the white hens were already in the garden. Flicka and Ricka went to get them grain to eat.

Dicka went to gather eggs.

"Perhaps there will be a golden brown one," she said.

But every day the girls found only white eggs.

"Maisie won't lay eggs for us," said Ricka. "Maybe she will, later."

Dicka went to gather eggs.

One morning, Flicka, Ricka, and Dicka went into the house and gave Mother the white eggs from the hens.

Suddenly, they heard a terrible noise from the garden. They all ran out to see what was happening.

They were just in time to see a big hawk try to catch Maisie in his claws. Maisie screeched at the hawk and flapped her wings. But when the girls and Mother shouted and waved their arms, the hawk flew away to the woods.

Once he was gone, Maisie shook her feathers and walked away as if nothing had happened.

Maisie screeched and flapped her wings.

The next morning, the girls went to feed the hens.

"Let's count them," said Ricka.

"Yes," said Flicka. "One, two, three, four, five—but where is Maisie?"

"I do hope she has not run away!" said Mother, who had just come into the garden.

They all began to search for Maisie. They looked behind the garden shed and in the bushes. Maisie was nowhere to be found.

"Perhaps the hawk has taken her," said Dicka.

Mother shook her head. "How could the hawk carry off a heavy hen like Maisie?" she said.

They all began to search for Maisie.

Every day, the girls took care of the chickens and collected the eggs that the five other hens laid.

But Maisie was gone. Every day they looked for her but could not find her.

At night, while they got ready for bed, they talked about her.

"How big and strong she was," said Flicka, "and how smart!"

"Remember how well she fought against the hawk?" said Dicka, beginning to cry.

"What will Aunt Lotta say when she hears about Maisie?" said Ricka.

How sad they were when they thought about Maisie!

How sad they were!

Many days had gone by since Maisie disappeared.

One day, the girls were sitting on a box behind the shed watching the hens.

"Soon we will have to return the chickens to Aunt Lotta," said Flicka.

"But how can we return just five hens," said Dicka. "And—" Her eyes grew big with wonder. She pointed to the bushes and said, "What is that moving under the bushes?"

For slowly coming out from under a bush was something red and yellow.

"Maisie! Maisie!" Flicka, Ricka, and Dicka shouted with joy. "Maisie has come back to us!"

"Maisie! Maisie!"

But Maisie did not come alone. Moving along beside her were six yellow fluffy baby chicks!

Mother came rushing from the house when she heard the shouting.

She began to laugh when she saw Maisie and her family. "Now I understand why she went away," Mother said. "We must find something for Maisie and her chicks to eat."

"What shall we give them for their breakfast?" asked the girls.

"We will give them some soft corn and dry, rolled oats," said Mother as she hurried to the kitchen.

Mother came rushing from the house.

At last, the day came for Flicka, Ricka, and Dicka to return the hens and rooster to Aunt Lotta.

Mother followed the girls, carrying the baby chicks in a big wicker basket.

Aunt Lotta, who did not know about Maisie's chicks, was very surprised to see them.

"These will be roosters and hens soon," she said, smiling. "I will save all of them for your very own."

"I hope one of the hens will be big and red," said Flicka.

"Then we can call her Maisie, too," said Dicka, and they all laughed happily.

Aunt Lotta was very surprised.